Gospel TimeTrekkers

Courageous Quest

Written by Maria Grace Dateno, FSP
Illustrated by Paul Cunningham

Pauline
BOOKS & MEDIA
Boston

Library of Congress Cataloging-in-Publication Data

Dateno, Maria Grace.
  Courageous quest / written by Maria Grace Dateno, FSP ; illustrated by
Paul Cunningham.
      pages cm. -- (Gospel time trekkers ; 5)
  Summary: Siblings Hannah, Caleb, and Noah travel through time and
space on a journey that retraces Jesus restoring Bartimaeus' sight and
calling Zacchaeus down from the tree.
  ISBN-13: 978-0-8198-1628-3
  ISBN-10: 0-8198-1628-0
  [1. Time travel--Fiction. 2. Brothers and sisters--Fiction. 3. Jesus Christ-
-Fiction. 4. Healing of the man born blind (Miracle)--Fiction. 5. Zac-
chaeus (Biblical figure)--Fiction. 6. Christian life--Fiction.] I. Cunning-
ham, Paul (Paul David), 1972- illustrator. II. Title.
  PZ7.D2598Co 2014
  [Fic]--dc23
                                    2013013466

The Scripture quotations contained herein are from the *New Revised Standard Version Bible: Catholic Edition*, copyright © 1989, 1993, Division of Christian Education of the National Council of the Churches of Christ in the United States of America. Used by permission. All rights reserved.

Cover design by Mary Joseph Peterson, FSP

Cover art by Paul Cunningham

All rights reserved. No part of this book may be reproduced or transmitted in any form or by any means, electronic or mechanical, including photocopying, recording, or by any information storage and retrieval system, without permission in writing from the publisher.

"P" and PAULINE are registered trademarks of the Daughters of St. Paul.

Copyright © 2014, Daughters of St. Paul

Published by Pauline Books & Media, 50 Saint Pauls Avenue, Boston, MA 02130-3491

Printed in the U.S.A.

CQ KSEUSAHUDNHA10-231011 1628-0

www.pauline.org

Pauline Books & Media is the publishing house of the Daughters of St. Paul, an international congregation of women religious serving the Church with the communications media.

1 2 3 4 5 6 7 8 9   17 16 15 14

*To my
(so far) twenty-two nieces and nephews,
who were my inspiration
for writing this series.*

Contents

Chapter One

Along for the Ride

I sat moping in the house on a Wednesday afternoon. It was a perfect September day. I had finished my school work early, and I was dying to go out, but I was stuck inside because of Garrett.

Garrett is our neighbor's little boy, almost two years old. My mom always watches him on Wednesdays. Each week, one of us (me, my eleven-year-old sister Hannah, or my six-year-old brother Noah) takes a turn watching him for a half-hour, while my mom does other stuff. He's a really cute kid, but the problem was, I couldn't bring him outside because he has allergies.

"Cabe," said Garrett. That's what he calls me because he can't say my name, Caleb.

I patted his head. He has silky, soft brown hair.

"Cabe pway." Garrett looked a little sad, like he didn't understand why I was just sitting there.

"Sorry, Garrett," I said. "I'm just mad at your allergies. What do you want to play?"

For an answer, he started pulling books off the bottom bookshelf in the living room and dropping them on the floor.

I dumped out a box of blocks and started building a tower to distract him. It worked. He came over and knocked down the tower.

I didn't say it to Garrett, but I wasn't just angry at his allergies. I felt angry at Hannah and Noah because they got to go outside. I knew it was my turn to watch Garrett this week, but I wished it were one of theirs.

I started piling the blocks again, this time faster.

Of course, Hannah and Noah didn't want to stay inside either, so they were probably *glad* it was my turn.

Garrett knocked the tower down again, giggling like crazy. I quickly built up four small ones in a row. But at that moment, I heard the back door open.

"Caleb?" called Hannah.

"We're in the living room."

I was surprised to see Hannah and Noah come around the corner.

"You know, Noah and I were thinking that maybe we would come in and hang out with you and Garrett."

"Really?" I said. I couldn't believe they would do that, when they could be outside having fun.

"We know how it's kind of boring playing with Garrett by yourself," said Hannah.

"Yeah," said Noah. "Let's ask Mom if we can get out something like clay or finger paints."

"Um, clay would be good, Noah," said Hannah, looking at Garrett. "Finger paints, not so much."

"Cay!" said Garrett. He sounded happy about playing with clay.

"Mom's doing laundry downstairs," I said.

Hannah picked up Garrett and we all walked toward the kitchen, where the basement stairs are.

And *that's* when it happened!

As we walked, we were suddenly moving in slow motion, and the air felt as thick as water.

And the next second, we were standing in an empty street, dressed in robes tied with belts around the waist. They're called tunics.

We weren't as surprised as you might think. This had happened before. Actually, it happens whenever we go back in time to the time of Jesus. Of course, we weren't expecting it at that moment!

"Oh no!" said Noah.

I looked at him in surprise. Usually when we realize we are on another adventure, Noah is jumping up and down for joy. This time he was standing there, with his mouth open, like something bad had happened.

Chapter Two

Making a Plan

I looked at what Noah was looking at.

It was Hannah. She was holding Garrett!

"Garrett came too?"

"Yeah, I guess because I was carrying him."

"Cool! Maybe next time I can bring my friend Kevin. I can't pick him up, but if he has his hand on my shoulder or something like that maybe—"

"Caleb, that's not going to work," said Hannah. "Kevin can't walk around with you for weeks. We never know when it's going to happen. It might *never* happen again."

"Oh, don't say that, Hannah!" said Noah. "I want it to keep on happening! I want to see Jesus!"

"Yeah, that's what we try to do every time, but we still haven't had a chance to see him," I said. "We need to find out where he is, right away, so we have time to travel there."

"It's true, the last two times we just missed him when he arrived in the town we were in. Remember in Gennesaret, he was arriving that morning and we were going to see him."

"And last time, in Capernaum, we were on our way to the place they said he was," said Noah.

"Hey, we know we have two nights here, right?" I said.

"Yeah," said Noah and Hannah together.

"So, let's plan how we will spend the time. We have the rest of today."

We all looked up at the sky. It seemed to be sometime in the afternoon.

"And all day tomorrow," said Hannah.

Garrett started squirming, and Hannah let him down.

"And a little bit of the next day," said Noah.

We had realized that all our adventures were the same length as the first one. They always ended on what Benjamin, the shepherd we met the first time, called the "third day." I was confused when he said it. We would say "two days later." But they counted it like the day we arrived was the first day, then the second day, then the third day.

"Okay, so today we will find someone who has some idea of where Jesus might be right now," I said. "Then tomorrow we will go there, and the 'third day' we will see him. How's that for a plan?"

Hannah and Noah smiled.

"Sounds good," said Hannah. "*If* Jesus is anywhere nearby."

"Well, he might be," said Noah hopefully.

"That's right. He might be. So let's do our best to find him," I said.

"I wonder where we are, first of all," said Hannah. "We've never been in the same place twice, so this is most likely a new town."

"It seems bigger," said Noah.

Hannah took Garrett's hand. He had been playing happily in the dirt.

We began walking down the small street we were on and came to a larger street. We could see several people down the street, all heading away from us.

"Let's go that way," I said.

We walked down the street a bit, but soon Garrett was tired. How did we know? He just sat down!

"Too bad we don't have a stroller," said Noah.

"Wa-wa!" whined Garrett.

"Oh, boy," said Noah. "How do we explain to him that we don't have water with us?"

"Usually there is a public well in the marketplace, right?" I said. "How about Noah and I go find it and you watch Garrett?"

Hannah looked at me.

"Are you sure that's a good idea? Maybe you two should stay with Garrett and I should go."

"No, I don't think any of us should go off

by ourselves," I said. "You watch Garrett and I'll watch Noah."

"I don't need watching!" said Noah. "You act like I'm a baby like Garrett."

Hannah and I looked at each other.

"No, Noah, you're not a baby like Garrett," I said. "I just meant that we should stay together and not go off by ourselves."

"Okay, fine," said Hannah. "Garrett and I will sit over there. You go find some water, and ask someone the name of the town, too."

"Okay," we said.

Noah and I set off down the street in the direction we had seen the people go. There were some palm trees on one side of the street. I hadn't seen any in any of the towns we had been in before. We passed houses made of stone that were a lot taller than the houses we had seen other times. Some of these were big, two stories tall, with walls around their yards. I guessed that the people here were richer than in the small towns we had visited before.

The marketplace was definitely bigger, too. Noah and I walked by people selling food and cloth and pots and jewelry and all kinds of things.

I stopped to watch a man looking at a roll of cloth that was a dark reddish-brown.

"Sir, look at this lovely dyed wool fabric," the merchant was saying to him. "This is the *finest* I have seen for a long time!"

"Hmm," said the man, feeling the material. "It is all right. How much is it?"

"Just *ten* of the coins you are clinking in your purse there, sir. Quite a bargain!"

"What! Ten? Surely you are not serious? I would never pay more than five!"

"But sir, this is woven from *very special* wool. It is from *Bethlehem* sheep. They are descendants of the *very sheep* that our noble ancestor David pastured near that great city."

"Sheep are very plentiful near Bethlehem. And King David lived a thousand years ago. Even if you were sure of the lineage of these sheep, that is no reason to cheat a hard-working man!"

"My friend, I understand that your money is well earned. For you, I will only charge nine. That is an *excellent* price for such quality material."

"I will give you seven, no more than that."

"Sir, I, too, work hard for my money! I travel the long distances between city and village. Otherwise people would not have these *excellent* goods. I will sell it to you for eight. That is my final price."

"Done. Here are your eight coins," said the man, and he handed the coins over to the merchant.

"That's funny," I said. "He ended up paying the amount right between what he said he would pay and what the merchant said it cost!"

I turned to Noah to see what he thought, and that's when I noticed that he wasn't next to me.

Chapter Three

Leah at the Well

I looked around, thinking maybe he was at another stand nearby, but I couldn't see him.

"Noah!" I called, searching the crowd around me. "Noah!"

Suddenly the marketplace seemed a very dangerous place, with many things that could happen to a small boy.

I thought of having to go back to Hannah and tell her that I had lost Noah. Even though Noah said he wasn't a baby, he *did* need watching. I was responsible for him.

"Noah!" I turned around in a circle, trying

to spot Noah's head among the people walking around the market. He and I both have very short, sand-colored hair. No one there had hair like ours.

I walked down to the end of the row I was in, and then back the other way. Just when I was thinking I'd have to ask someone for help, I spotted him. He was standing in the next row over, looking at the vegetables a man was selling.

"Noah!" I said as I came up behind him. "Where were you?"

"What do you mean? I was right here."

"Don't wander off like that," I said.

"I didn't wander off. I was right here the whole time!"

"Well, keep close to me," I said. "I'm responsible for you, so I don't want you going off without me!"

We walked through more of the market and came to the public well, where everyone gets their water.

I picked up one of the jugs they have there for people to use, then waited for my turn to haul up some water.

"Son, do you want me to fill that for you?"

I looked at the woman who had just pulled up a bucket of water. She looked about the age of my mom, or maybe a little older. She had a brown tunic and a brown mantle, which is a scarf-like thing people wear on their heads. She was smiling and holding the bucket out toward me, like she wanted me to let her pour the water into my jug.

"Oh, you go ahead," I said. "We can get our own."

"I have enough," she replied. "Let me fill yours."

"Thanks!" I said. "We need to bring this over to our sister and the baby she's watching. Is it all right if we take the jug out of the market square and bring it back soon?"

"Yes, you may take it, as long as you bring it back," she said as she poured the water.

Noah and I had a drink of water. And then, since this lady seemed so nice, I decided to ask her for information.

"Excuse me," I said. "Can you tell us the name of this place?"

"What? You do not know the name of this city?" asked the lady. Her eyebrows went way up like she couldn't believe I didn't know. "This is Jericho!" Her eyebrows went down as she frowned. "How did you get here? Where are your parents?"

"They're in Maryland," said Noah. "We got here just by walking through the living room!"

"What?" said the lady.

"Nothing, never mind," I said. "Our parents are far away from here—we don't really know how we got here," I said. I realized how stupid that sounded, even though it was true, so I quickly added, "We're looking for Jesus. Do you know if he comes here sometimes?"

The woman smiled a huge smile.

"Yes! He came through just a couple of days ago," she said. "He came here, and now everything is different!"

"Do you think he will come back again in the next couple of days?"

"Oh, no. He was on his way up to Jerusalem."

"Well, we'd better be getting along. We

have to bring this to our sister. But thank you for the water and for telling us about Jesus."

"You are welcome. What are your names?"

"I'm Caleb."

"I'm Noah."

"My name is Leah. See that street there? I live in a little house near the end of it. My house is next door to the big house with the three palm trees in the courtyard. Come there if you need a place to stay."

"Thanks!" I said.

"That's very nice of you!" said Noah.

We went as quickly as we could without spilling the jug of water. At one point, we passed some boys about my age and older, who were hanging out at the edge of the market. They looked at me and Noah and started laughing, pointing to our hair.

"Little old men!" I heard one of them saying.

Noah looked at me, like he didn't know what to do.

"Just ignore them," I said quietly.

It was true that I had not seen anyone on our time travel adventures with light-colored hair like ours. Almost everyone had dark brown or black hair. A lot of them had curly hair. No one had their hair cut like ours, either. But still, it was mean of them to laugh.

We finally turned the corner onto the street where Hannah said she would sit with little Garrett. Suddenly I had the scary thought that maybe Hannah and Garrett would be missing. Maybe they had gotten so thirsty that they had gone somewhere else to ask for water.

As we got closer to the palm trees, though, I could see Hannah was there. But even before that, I could hear Garrett. He was definitely not happy.

Chapter Four

Meeting Daniel

"Waaaaaaaaaaaah!" cried Garrett. "Waaaa aaaaaaaaaaaaaah!"

"Hi, Hannah," said Noah as we came up.

"Finally!" snapped Hannah. "Bring that jug of water over here!"

She wasn't being very nice, but I guess I couldn't blame her if Garrett had been screaming like that for a while.

It was hard to help Garrett drink from the jug, but after a bit, he had had enough and wasn't thirsty anymore, so he stopped crying.

Hannah drank after him, and then we all felt better.

"Hannah, I found out what city we're in—it's called Jericho," I said.

"Jericho? Like 'Joshua and the battle of Jericho'?" she asked.

"I guess. And I talked to a lady named Leah we met at the well. She said Jesus was here a couple of days ago! So we just missed him!"

"Maybe we can go wherever he went. Did you ask which direction he went in?"

"She said he was on his way up to Jerusalem," I said.

"Let's ask how to get there," said Noah.

"We need to find somewhere to stay tonight," said Hannah.

"Leah said we can stay at her house. I know where it is."

We started out toward the place she had described to me. Garrett walked for a while, but he was too slow. Hannah said he was too heavy to carry.

"Piggy-back is easier than carrying him in the front," I said. "Let me have him."

So I took him to give him a piggy-back ride for a while. We got to the well and put back the water jug. As we left, I noticed a boy watching us. He was one of the boys who was laughing at us before. But this time he was by himself. I ignored him as we walked by, but he called out after us.

"Hello there! Where are you from?'

"Hello," said Hannah. "We're travelers and we need a place to stay. Do you know where we could go?"

"Hannah, I told you we could go to that lady's house. She was very nice."

And I called over to the boy, "Never mind, I know someone's house we can go to."

But instead of leaving us alone, the boy came over.

"Whose house?" he asked.

"None of your business," I said.

"Caleb! What's gotten into you? Don't be so nasty," said Hannah.

But the boy didn't seem angry. He probably didn't know what "none of your business" meant.

"So your name is Caleb? Mine is Daniel. Do not let the boys' teasing bother you. They call me 'O Wise One' all the time. I just ignore them. And you must admit, your hair *is* strange looking."

"Yeah, well, it's not very nice to make fun of people just because their hair is different from yours," I said. "You should be kind."

Many times on our adventures, people had helped us and given us food and a place to stay. Back in the time of Jesus, people were very nice to strangers and travelers.

"You are right. I am sorry. Now, let me help you find a place to stay. Are you going to the house of Leah?"

"How did you know?" asked Noah.

"I saw you talking to her at the well."

"Oh."

"Daniel, do you know where her house is? Maybe you could take us there," said Hannah.

"I *know* where it is, Hannah," I said. Why did she think we needed help from this kid? He didn't look any older than her.

"I can certainly take you there," said Daniel. "And what are your names?" he asked.

"I'm Hannah, and this is Garrett."

"Hello, Garrett," said Daniel, patting Garrett's head. "What a funny-sounding name."

"And I'm Noah."

"Welcome, Noah."

"Let's go to Leah's house," said Hannah. "Garrett is tired and hungry."

"Here, let me carry him," said Daniel.

"Do you know if we could borrow a stroller somewhere?" asked Noah.

"A what?"

"Nothing. Never mind," I said. "I've got him." He *was* pretty heavy, though.

"Let me take him for a while," said Daniel. He took Garrett from me and put him on his shoulders.

"Up!" said Garrett, with a big smile on his face. He didn't act like that when I gave him a piggy-back ride. And riding on someone's shoulders isn't *that* much higher up than riding on someone's back.

"Carrying him is nothing compared with the work of reaping all day," said Daniel, as

Garrett began playing with his curly brown hair.

"Why were you weeping all day?" asked Noah.

"Ha! Not 'weeping'—*reaping*!" said Daniel.

"What's reaping?" asked Noah.

"It means cutting the wheat. Reaping, threshing, and winnowing are the steps of the wheat harvest."

"What's threshing?" asked Noah.

I was glad Noah asked, because I wanted to know too, but I didn't want Daniel to know I didn't know.

"Threshing is what gets the grains of wheat off the stems they grow on. And it takes the outer husk off the grain. The threshers spread the wheat out on the threshing floor and the oxen pull the threshing sled over it.

"And since I am sure you also will ask what winnowing is, I will tell you that, too. The outer husk that has been cracked off the grains of wheat is called chaff. The winnower tosses the wheat and chaff into the air. The chaff is lighter, so the wind blows it away. The grains of wheat are heavier and they fall back to the ground, where they are gathered.

"It is funny that you do not know anything about harvesting wheat," said Daniel.

"We have a vegetable garden at home," said Hannah. "But we don't grow wheat or things like that."

"Our father is a carpenter," I said, to explain why we wouldn't know about farming. But even if we did, I was pretty sure that farmers used machines to do all those steps nowadays.

"What does your father do?" asked Noah. "Is he a farmer?"

"I do not have a father," said Daniel. And for the first time, I saw his smile disappear. "He died when I was only a baby. It is just my mother and I."

Chapter Five

Dinner on the Roof

"Oh, sorry," said Noah.

I felt bad, too. It must be very hard not to have a father. Especially back at the time of Jesus, when boys usually learned from their fathers whatever kind of work they did. I wondered what a boy did when he had no father.

"I'm sorry to hear that, Daniel," said Hannah.

Daniel stopped and pulled Garrett down off his shoulders. I saw the big house with the three palm trees that Leah had mentioned. And next to it was a very small stone house. Daniel looked at us with a little smile.

"Here we are," said Daniel. "Imma, we're here!" he called out.

Hannah and I looked at each other. Imma? We had learned on another trip that "Abba" meant "Dad" and "Imma" meant . . . "Mom."

"Daniel? Is Leah your *mother*?" asked Hannah.

Daniel smiled big.

"Yes, she sent me to look for you after she talked to your brothers at the well."

Hannah laughed.

"Why didn't you say something?"

I felt a little annoyed that he had tricked us like that, but it was hard to feel angry with someone who had just said his father was dead. And he *had* been very nice to help us and carry Garrett.

The door of the house opened and Leah was standing there.

"Ah, good. You found them. Run and get another loaf of bread at the baker's, Daniel."

You'd think he would have been mad about having to do more chores because of us, but Daniel ran off, still smiling.

"Come, children," said Leah. "Come inside and rest."

"Thank you so much, Leah," said Hannah. "We really appreciate a place to stay tonight."

"Now I met Caleb and Noah already, but what are your names?" asked Leah when we were all inside. There was only one room in the house, and it seemed to be the kitchen. There was something that smelled good in a pot over a fire.

Garrett immediately started whining.

"Mm! Mac!" he said.

Uh-oh. "Mac" was how he said "macaroni and cheese." I didn't think we'd be able to find any of that around here.

"This is Garrett," said Hannah. "He's our neighbor's baby that we're taking care of. My name is Hannah. Can I help you with dinner?"

"Dinner is all ready. I am sure you must all be hungry. I can tell Garrett is," said Leah, picking him up. "There is plenty of lentil stew for everyone. And Daniel will be back with another loaf of bread. This one I made from the grain I gleaned from the fields yesterday."

We went out of the house and up a skinny stairway on the side. It led to the roof of the house. Leah pointed out the things you could see from up there. The house next door belonged to a man named Zacchaeus. In another direction we could see fields beyond the houses. There was a kind of little wall around the edge of the roof, but still, it wouldn't take much for Garrett to climb over and fall off.

The food was very good. Luckily Garrett liked it, too. He sat in Hannah's lap and ate happily and messily. Daniel came back with the bread and sat down.

"Daniel explained about the wheat harvest," said Hannah. "But he didn't mention 'gleaning.' You said you gleaned the grain from the fields. What does that mean, Leah?"

"A widow like me is allowed to go into the fields after the reapers have finished. We are allowed to glean—to collect the wheat that is left behind. That is part of God's law, so that the poor will have wheat, too."

Daniel looked at his mother. It seemed like he was a little embarrassed, but I didn't understand why.

"Daniel works very hard," Leah said, smiling at him. "But every little bit helps."

"Oh," said Hannah.

I think she was feeling the same thing I was. I felt bad for eating the little bit of bread she had. And how could they afford to go buy another loaf for us, too?

Leah must have known what we were thinking.

"Do not worry," she said, breaking off another piece of bread for Garrett. "We have plenty right now. Eat and enjoy it."

"So, you came here to find Jesus?" asked Daniel, changing the subject.

"Yes," said Hannah. "We were disappointed that he already left for Jerusalem."

"Everyone going up to Jerusalem for Passover has gone already," said Leah.

"Have you ever gone to Jerusalem for Passover?" asked Hannah.

"A few times when I was much younger," said Leah, looking a little sad. "Daniel has never gone."

"Why?" I asked. "How far is it to Jerusalem from here?"

"It is not that far," said Daniel. "It would not take even one day to walk there. But I have no time to go traveling."

Hannah looked like she felt bad for Daniel. But I was excited about one thing—he said it would not take even one day to walk to Jerusalem. That meant we could go tomorrow and see Jesus!

"Besides," continued Daniel, "I have seen amazing things right here in Jericho. Something most people in Jerusalem have never seen."

Chapter Six

Daniel's Story

"What?" asked Noah. "What have you seen that most people have never seen?"

Leah smiled at Daniel.

"Just tell them *your* story. We'll get Zacchaeus to tell them *his* story tomorrow, okay?" she said. "And you can go ahead and start while I wash Garrett up and put him to bed."

Garrett was rubbing his eyes like he was very tired. As he did that, he rubbed the lentil stew around on his face.

"Oh, Leah, I can do that," said Hannah.

"No, dear, I haven't had a baby boy to hold for a long time. It would be my pleasure. He can sleep inside with me, too. You can sleep up here, but it's not safe for a little one like Garrett."

"It was in the morning," began Daniel, "and I was working in the fields of Jacob. We were reaping the grain. At one point, we saw a crowd of people coming down the road. Someone ran over to find out who it was, and came back to say it was the teacher, Jesus. Most of us left the field to follow him into town. Jesus had been through before and people knew he could heal the sick. I had something I wanted his help with, but since it was not a sickness, I did not know if he could help me."

"What did you want help with?" asked Noah.

"I will tell you later in the story," said Daniel. "Right now I want to tell you about the most amazing thing I ever saw in my life."

Hannah and Noah and I smiled at each other. I think we were all remembering the other times on our adventures when someone said something like that before telling us a story about Jesus. I felt a little squirming in my stomach like you feel when you are looking forward to something fun. Funny that I should feel so excited about just hearing a story.

"As the crowd walked down the road that leads into the city," continued Daniel, "there was a man by the side of the road, begging. I have known him my whole life. His name is Bartimaeus, and he was blind. He couldn't have seen who was walking by, but he must have asked someone in the front of the crowd. He started shouting for Jesus. He kept calling out, 'Jesus, son of David, have pity on me!'

"Why did he call him 'son of David'?" asked Noah.

"Well, you know that when the Savior comes he will be of the house of David. I guess Bartimaeus knew Jesus could save him, so he called him that," said Daniel.

"Did Jesus go and heal him?" Noah asked.

"He probably did not even hear him at first, because of the noise the crowd was making. The people who were passing by Bartimaeus kept telling him to be quiet. But he kept shouting. I have never seen him like that. He is usually very quiet and just asks for alms when he hears footsteps going by him."

We had learned on one of our adventures that "alms" meant money or food given to the poor. I was glad we didn't have to ask what it meant.

"I was curious," continued Daniel. "So I squeezed through the people to get closer to Bartimaeus. I was nearby when someone said, 'Get up. Jesus is calling for you.'

"Bartimaeus stood up immediately. He had a cloak wrapped around him, which he just dropped to the ground as he went toward Jesus. I was surprised that he left his cloak behind. I was sure it was the only one he had, and he might not find it again. I wanted to go pick it up so it wouldn't get lost or trampled. But I lost track of it in the crowd.

"Bartimaeus rushed forward to Jesus, with people helping to guide him. Then Jesus asked something that surprised me. Jesus said to him, 'What do you want me to do for you?'"

"But Jesus could tell he was blind," said Hannah. "I wonder why he would ask that."

"I do not know," said Daniel. "But Bartimaeus just said, 'Lord, I want to see!' And Jesus said, 'Receive your sight.' And Bartimaeus could see—just like that!"

Daniel stopped and shook his head.

"I still can hardly believe it, and I saw it with my own eyes. He made a blind man see! It is impossible to make someone blind be able to see just by saying words. But Jesus did it. And Bartimaeus jumped up and shouted even louder than before, 'Oh! I can see!' And he fell on his knees in front of Jesus and kind of hugged his feet. Then he jumped up and kept saying, 'I can see! I can see!' as he ran around looking at everything."

"Did you find his cloak?" I asked.

Daniel laughed. "No, I went over to tell him that I had tried to get it for him. He did not know me, of course. But I had given him alms many times. When he heard my voice, he recognized that, and he gave me a hug.

"I don't need my cloak anymore," he said. "But thank you!"

"After that, I was hoping even more that I could ask Jesus to help me. But there were so many people crowding around as word got to the city that Jesus was here. I could not get close to him."

"Why didn't you just wait? Maybe later that day or the next morning, there would have been fewer people around Jesus," said Hannah.

Leah came back to sit with us at that point.

"Usually pilgrims just go through the city," she explained. "if they arrive early enough in the day. It was not even noon. If they continued straight through like many pilgrims do, they could arrive at Jerusalem that evening."

"So," continued Daniel, "I decided to run ahead by going down another street and cutting across to where Jesus would pass. Then instead of trying to get through the crowd, *I* would be in front."

Chapter Seven

Hope and Disappointment

"That was a good idea!" said Noah.

"Yes, it was, but someone else thought of it before me. I was waiting at a corner, and Jesus was almost there. But all of a sudden, he stopped; then he looked up. He was standing under a sycamore tree, and there was a man up in the tree! Jesus looked at him and said, 'Hurry down, Zacchaeus. I am staying at your house today!'

"Then, while Zacchaeus was climbing down from the tree, Jesus looked over and saw me standing at the corner. He looked at me for a moment—I mean, really looked into my eyes. Then he smiled a gentle smile. I could not help it—I smiled back at him. Suddenly, I was sure that everything would be fine. He did not say anything, but I did not feel worried anymore.

"It only took a minute—just the time it took for Zacchaeus to come down from the tree. I did not stay to see what else happened because I turned around and walked back to the fields."

Daniel stopped. I waited a second, then asked, "So, what happened? What was it you wanted Jesus to help you with?"

"I told you my father is dead," explained Daniel. "I need to find someone to teach me a trade—someone to accept me as an apprentice. I would love to be a coppersmith or a potter. I am willing to learn any honorable work. But my mother and I owe some people money. I have to keep working to pay it back and to support us."

"Did Jesus help you with that?" I asked.

"Not yet, but I know it will turn out all right. That is what his smile said to me."

After Leah and Daniel said good night, Hannah, Noah, and I lay on the roof. We talked about our plans. The next morning, we would ask for some food for our trip.

"But I feel bad to ask Leah," said Hannah. "They have so little. And they have debts, too."

"They have *deaths*?" asked Noah.

"Debts—it means they owe money."

"And even though Daniel has to work very hard, he said he had given money to that blind man many times," I said.

"Yes, they are generous, but I still don't like to ask."

"Maybe she knows someone who would share with us," I said. "This neighbor, Zacchaeus, might."

"She wants us to hear his story, so we could go over there early tomorrow to hear his story, and we might be able to ask for some bread and cheese to take with us," said Hannah.

"And then we'll walk to Jerusalem," said Noah.

"We can ask Zacchaeus directions, too," I said. "I'm sure he knows the way there."

"And when we get to Jerusalem, we'll ask someone where Jesus is," said Noah.

"And we could ask Zacchaeus if he knows where we could stay in Jerusalem," said Hannah. "It's a big place, I'm sure. Bigger than anywhere else we've been."

"And then we'll finally get to see Jesus!" said Noah excitedly.

"If everything goes as planned, Noah," said Hannah.

We lay there silently for a bit, just feeling happy about our plans. And eventually we all fell asleep.

The next morning, Daniel had already gone out to work in the fields by the time we woke up and had breakfast. Breakfast was a mushy thing like oatmeal, but made from wheat. Noah and I didn't like it very much, but Hannah did. And Garrett sat on Leah's lap and ate it all up like he loved it.

As we were finishing, Hannah and I looked at each other, and she nodded.

"Leah," I said. "We need some bread and cheese to take with us on our trip. If you don't have any extra right now, maybe you know who we could ask?"

"We thought perhaps Zacchaeus," said Hannah.

"We need to leave for Jerusalem this morning," I said. "Because we don't have much time here and we really want to see Jesus."

"Wait!" said Leah. "How are you going to go to Jerusalem? I told you that everyone has gone by now. There may be a group of pilgrims coming through but I doubt they would take you."

"We'll just go by ourselves," said Noah.

"What?" said Leah. "No, you cannot go by yourselves!"

"Why not?" asked Hannah.

"It's too far for you to walk by yourselves."

"We've walked from Sogane to Cana in Galilee in one day—in a thunderstorm," I said. "It can't be much farther." That had happened in our second adventure.

"But you will get lost."

"We will get good directions," said Hannah. "We understood there was a road that goes straight there."

"But it is too dangerous!" said Leah.

"What's dangerous about it?" I asked.

"Have you not heard about all the robbers that attack travelers on that road? Imagine—children going by themselves from Jericho to Jerusalem! It is uphill all the way, too."

"I don't think they would attack us," I said. "We won't have anything with us that would look like it was valuable."

"And we can run very fast!" said Noah.

"*You* can run fast. But Garrett cannot. And you cannot run fast while you are carrying him!"

Chapter Eight

So Close,
Yet So Far Away

"Oh! Garrett!" exclaimed Hannah.

"Garrett!" Noah echoed.

I couldn't believe we had forgotten him. It would definitely be a hard trip with Garrett.

"Yes, Garrett," said Leah.

"Oh, but we have to go to Jerusalem. We just *have* to," said Noah. "Maybe you could watch Garrett for us. We really have to see Jesus today!"

"Noah, we can't leave Garrett here in Jericho," said Hannah.

"I could take care of him for a few days," said Leah. "But you cannot go to Jerusalem by

45

yourselves. Three children walking that road, with no protection? With the robbers so bad this year? No. I am sorry to disappoint you. You must wait until you can find a caravan."

We all sat there and didn't answer.

"Why not go out and explore Jericho a little? You can see the palaces of King Herod up on the hill. I need to run some errands. We can go visit Zacchaeus later."

So Hannah took Garrett and washed his face and we went out for a walk.

"Noah, what were you thinking?" I asked. "We can't leave Garrett. What if we're not back tomorrow morning?"

"We definitely wouldn't be back tomorrow morning if we left for Jerusalem today," said Hannah.

"Garrett is our responsibility," I said.

"He's *your* responsibility," said Noah. "It was *your* turn to watch him."

"Nah?" said Garrett. That's how he says Noah's name. He looked confused.

Noah looked at Garrett, then looked away angrily.

"But we are all here together now," said Hannah.

"Anyway, you and Hannah said you would help me. It's not my fault this adventure happened in the middle of my half-hour turn of watching Garrett!"

"Anyway," said Hannah. "The robbers make things impossible, even if we didn't have Garrett. The three of us can't go by ourselves down a road with that kind of danger."

We walked around a little, and we could see some of the palace buildings up on the hill. But it was too far for Garrett to walk, and he was too heavy to carry that far.

Noah walked around with a frown on his face. I could tell he was angry about not being able to go.

"Noah, it's not going to do any good to act like this. We just have to accept it and hope that we can come again," I said.

He didn't say anything, but just pouted even more.

"Caleb, why don't you and Noah go a little closer to the palaces and see those palm trees over there?" said Hannah. "I can stay here with Garrett for a while."

"I don't want to see the stupid trees," said Noah.

"Fine, stay here with Hannah and the baby!" I said.

That made Noah come with me, as I knew it would.

"If we're not here when you come back," said Hannah. "We'll have gone back to Leah's house, okay?" Garrett was picking up handfuls of dirt and throwing them.

There wasn't much to see, but soon we came upon a group of about eight or ten men. As we got closer, I saw they had two donkeys with bundles tied on their backs. And the men had walking sticks.

"Hey, look!" said Noah. "Those people look like they're going on a trip. Let's ask where they're going." He hurried over to them. As I caught up with him, he was already asking his question.

"We are going to Jerusalem, son," said a man with a brown and white tunic and a white mantle over his head.

"Oh! We didn't think there were any more people going to Jerusalem," said Noah.

"We actually started two days ago," said the man. "But we had to turn back after being attacked by robbers. We are going to try again today. Now we are better armed and can protect ourselves."

"Oh! Can we come?" said Noah. "Please?"

"Noah, we can't go to Jerusalem. We already talked about this."

Noah frowned at me.

"I'm sorry," I said to the group. "My brother is very young. He doesn't understand that we can't go."

Noah made a face at me.

"We wouldn't be any trouble," said Noah. "We can walk very fast and not get tired!"

"Noah! That's enough!"

"We would not mind your coming, but I am sure your parents would," said another man, smiling.

"We can't go," I said. "We have to stay with my older sister and a little baby we're taking care of."

"Oh, no, we definitely do not want any babies along," said the first man.

"Sorry to bother you. Have a good trip," I said, pulling Noah away.

"Caleb! They said we could go!"

"Noah! Listen! We cannot leave Garrett."

"But Leah would watch him."

"You know what happens on the third day, Noah."

"I know—we go back home. But we go back from wherever we are. Garrett would too. It probably wouldn't make any difference if he wasn't with us," he said.

"'Probably' is not good enough," I said. "I really want to see Jesus, too. But how would you feel if Hannah and I decided to leave *you* behind? Now, come on. Let's see what's down this street."

"No! I want to go to Jerusalem!" said Noah, stamping his foot.

"Noah, stop acting like a baby!"

Noah made a face at me, but he followed me down the street. I soon noticed a banging sound. It turned out to be a smith's workshop. We stopped to watch a man hammering something. It was cool to see the sparks flying each time the hammer hit the metal thing he was making. Maybe Daniel would get a smith to teach him. We stood there for a long time, watching. At least I stood there for a long time. I don't know how long Noah stood there. Because when I turned to say something to him, he was gone.

Chapter Nine

Noah's Plan

"Noah?" I looked around on both sides of the street, but I didn't see him. "Ugh! Where is he?"

Boy, was I mad at him. He was more trouble than Garrett at this point. Just because he didn't get his way, he ran off. I stomped back down the street, looking around as I went. I asked a few people if they had seen a boy that looked like me, but smaller. No one had. I was hungry. It must have been time for lunch.

If he's hiding from me, I thought, *he's really going to get it*!

But after walking all the way past where the group of travelers had been, and back down the next street, I started to get worried.

Where could he be?

What should I do?

I could go back to find Hannah. But she had Garrett with her. We couldn't go very fast carrying him. And Noah had been my responsibility. I wanted to find him. I didn't want to have to tell Hannah that I had lost him.

But I had no idea where to look in this big place. He wasn't anywhere nearby. Unless he was hiding.

I walked around some more, calling for Noah. I ended back at the beginning of the street where the travelers had been. I stopped and just stood there, not knowing what to do.

What if I never found him? What if he had been kidnapped? What would happen on the third day when we went back home?

The thing was, I knew it was my fault. I had known that Noah was mad about not going to Jerusalem, but I made it worse by what I said to him. I didn't look after him well.

I couldn't help it—I started crying.

That's when I heard someone say:

"Hello there, child. What is wrong?

I looked up and saw an old man. His tunic looked kind of dirty, and it was torn in a few places. He had white hair and bushy white eyebrows, and carried a walking stick. But his eyes looked kind.

He was looking at me in a concerned way.

"My name is Bartimaeus," he said. "What is your name?"

"I'm Caleb. I'm looking for my little brother. I lost him!"

"Oh," said Bartimaeus. "By any chance, does your little brother have light-colored hair like yours, also cut short and sticking up?"

"Yes! Have you seen him?"

"I did. A while ago I saw him walking down the road. Now that I can see, I feel responsible to use my eyes well. I was surprised to see a young child by himself on the road leading to Jerusalem. I called to him, but he was too far and did not hear me. But then I saw a small caravan ahead of him on the road. I guessed that he was with them."

"No! He was not supposed to be with them! Which way did he go?"

"Come, I will show you."

We went as fast as he could go, which wasn't fast enough for me. He pointed out the road to me.

I was about to run off, but Bartimaeus stopped me.

"Wait. I'm not fast enough to go with you. But I can tell your family what has happened. Where are you staying?"

I told him about Hannah and Garrett, and Leah's house. Then I ran off down the road. It led out of the city and across some fields and up into the hills. The hills were so brown and dry looking. It didn't take long for me to get out of breath because I had already been running around before and because I was still kind of crying.

I had to walk for a while, but I kept looking up the road, trying to see a little boy. How far ahead of me could he be? I had lost track of time completely.

When I thought about robbers, I ran.

When I couldn't run anymore, I walked.

I got across the fields and was just about to run into the hills, when I heard someone call out to me, "Hey, Caleb!"

I spun around and saw it was Daniel!

"Caleb, where are you going?"

"Oh, Daniel, I have to find Noah! He went off on his own!"

"Wait, Caleb. Stop and tell me what happened."

"I lost him, Daniel. I was supposed to be watching him. He really wanted to go to Jerusalem, but we can't."

I told him what had happened and what Bartimaeus had seen.

"Does anyone else know about this?" asked Daniel.

I told him Bartimaeus was going to find Hannah to tell her.

"Okay, let us go now," said Daniel.

"You're coming with me?" I said. I could hardly believe it. "Don't you have to be working in the fields?"

"Yes, but this is more important. We need

to find Noah before he comes to grief on the road."

I wasn't sure what "comes to grief" meant, but I thought it probably had something to do with getting lost, falling off a cliff, or being attacked by robbers.

Chapter Ten

Run for Your Lives!

It seemed like we were walking forever. Once we got to the hilly part, the road was almost always uphill. We walked and walked. Luckily, Daniel had some food in his bag. He called it "parched grains." It was grains of wheat that had been cooked and dried somehow. They were chewy, but good. And we could eat a handful as we walked. He had some water, too. It was in a bag-shaped container, like a kind of soft canteen. We each took a gulp.

"There isn't much. Let's save the rest for Noah," said Daniel.

As we walked, every once in a while we would stop. I would call Noah's name. Then we would be quiet and listen, to hear if he was calling back to us.

"Noah!" I called for the fourth or fifth time. "NO-AH!"

We stopped to listen. Nothing. Then a wonderful sound.

"Caleb? Caleb!"

Daniel and I ran toward where we heard it coming from. We went around a big rock and there was Noah, sitting on the ground, crying.

"Noah!" I yelled, and went to grab him and hug him.

"Caleb," said Noah, crying. "I'm hungry."

Daniel gave Noah some parched grain and the rest of the water. Then we started back. It was easier because the road wasn't uphill.

We were talking and laughing until I noticed Daniel's worried face.

"What's wrong?" I asked.

"I think we should be quiet, just in case," he said.

"Okay," I agreed.

So we walked quietly. That's when I heard a noise that made me stop in my tracks. I looked at Daniel and Noah, and I could tell they heard it too. It was the sound of voices, and it was coming closer.

"Let's hide," I said, and pointed to a chunk of rock that had been part of the cliff, but had broken off. We got behind it and could hear the voices getting louder.

"There are two of them," said Daniel as he peeked out from behind the rock. "They look like robbers."

They got closer, and we could hear the crunch of their feet on the road. Daniel put his finger to his lips.

"Over here is a good place," one of the robbers said.

"Yeah, there's that flat area," said the other. "And no one will be coming down the road. It's too late in the day."

The footsteps seemed closer and closer. The robbers were going off the road right next to us! Noah's eyes got really big as he realized what was happening.

What were we going to do? If we walked off down the road, they would see us if they were facing that direction. And they would hear us. I looked at Daniel. For the first time, he looked really scared. It didn't seem like he had a plan. I looked at Noah. I was afraid he would start crying and give us away.

I closed my eyes to think, but ended up praying instead. *Jesus, help us!* was all that came to me. Then suddenly, something else came—an idea.

I bent over and picked up a stone. Daniel looked at me with a question in his face. I faced toward the road going to Jerusalem and pretended to throw the stone. Daniel still didn't get it, so I turned toward the road back to Jericho and made motions like I was running. I could tell by his face that he got my idea.

I picked up another couple of stones. Daniel took Noah's hand and faced the way we would run—downhill, toward Jericho. I faced the other direction and got ready to throw my stones. The first one I threw as high and far as I could. I threw the next one right after it.

"What was that?" I heard one man say.

"Probably just an animal," said the other.

"We'd better check."

As they got up to go look, Daniel and Noah crept as quickly as they could down the road. I followed trying not to let my steps crunch on the dirt. We didn't have to go far before we were out of sight. We just had to go quickly and quietly.

After we went around the next bend, we started running. We ran until we couldn't run anymore. We collapsed onto a big flat rock. Noah was crying again. But Daniel was smiling.

"That was very smart," he said.

"Do you think they will come after us?" I asked.

"I do not know, but we should get going," said Daniel.

We hadn't gone very far when we heard voices again. But they were friendly!

"Caleb! Noah!" someone was calling.

We all looked at each other and then hurried toward the sound.

Chapter Eleven

The Man in the Tree

Bartimaeus had gone to Leah, who asked Zacchaeus for help. Zacchaeus had gotten a group of people to come look for us. One of them gave Noah a piggy-back ride home. Soon we were safely back in Jericho.

Hannah came running out of the house.

"You guys, I was so afraid!" she said, hugging us. Garrett seemed happy to see us, too.

"Nah! Cabe!" he said.

We had dinner at Zacchaeus's house that evening, along with Leah and Daniel.

His house was a lot different from Leah's. It

had two stories and a lot more rooms. The big courtyard had a high wall around it. There was a garden to one side and some palm trees. We ate in a big room on the upper floor.

Zacchaeus turned out to be very nice. He was a very short man with brown curly hair and a beard. His face was round, and when he smiled and laughed, he looked like a kid. Except for the beard, of course.

"Zacchaeus," said Leah, "these children came here hoping to see Jesus. They were very disappointed that he had gone. So I thought it would be nice for them to hear your story about him."

"So, you want to hear how I became a better person?" asked Zacchaeus.

"We want to hear what you were doing in the tree," said Noah.

Zacchaeus laughed.

"I was in the tree because I was curious. That is what I would have said if someone had asked me at that moment what I was doing. *Now* I understand that I was in the tree because I was searching for something. I thought I was happy with my money and my big house. But deep inside, I was not happy. I was searching for something that would fix that.

"I had gone for a walk that morning. I ran into a friend. He looked excited so I stopped to talk to him.

"'Did you hear about Bartimaeus?' he asked me.

"'Who?'

"'Bartimaeus, the blind beggar that you always see on the road coming into the city.'

"'No, what about him?'

"'Jesus cured him. He is not blind anymore. He can see. I definitely saw him seeing.'

"I laughed and said that maybe Bartimaeus has been fooling us all these years. The man frowned and shook his head. 'No, he was certainly blind!' he said. 'One time I saw him walk straight into a wall. Jesus healed him!'

"So that is what made me curious. I had heard about Jesus before, but I had never seen him. I really wanted to know what he looked like. I walked farther and saw a crowd. Now, you see how short I am. I could not see Jesus.

I did not want to squeeze through the crowd. I told myself that it would not be dignified."

"So you climbed a tree?" I said.

Zacchaeus laughed. "Yes. And that is not dignified, either, I know! But actually, I did it because I did not want to see Jesus face to face. I wanted to see *him*, but I did not want *him* to see *me*."

"Did you get a good look at Jesus?"

"Yes! I saw which way the crowd was heading. I ran ahead and climbed a sycamore tree—the one near the market. I watched as Jesus approached. He was smiling and talking to all the people near him. As he got closer, my feelings changed. I was wishing I could talk to him. I *wanted* him to look at me. Then when he got to the tree, he looked up!"

"So Jesus is the one who saw you?" I asked. "Not the people in the crowd?"

"Yes, Jesus looked up first. Then he said, 'Zacchaeus, hurry down. I mean to stay at your house today.'"

"How did he know your name?" asked Hannah.

"I do not know. I had never met him before. But I felt very honored that he had chosen my house. However, many of the people standing around were not happy. They did not think that Jesus should honor me in that way. And I had to admit that I was not a very good person. Suddenly I had the desire to be someone who could happily invite Jesus to my house. I felt bad about the many things I had done that I should not have done."

"Like what?" said Noah.

"Noah!" said Hannah.

"That is all right," said Zacchaeus. "I am happy to tell you how meeting Jesus has changed me. I was a tax collector. Do you know what that is?"

"Someone who collects taxes?" said Noah. "What's wrong with that?"

"The Romans tell the tax collector how much money he must give them. The collector is supposed to collect it from the people in the city, with a little extra to support himself. The more extra the tax collector collects, the more money he has. I collected a lot extra over the years."

"Oh," said Noah.

"The money that was making me rich actually belonged to many of the people there in the crowd. So I stood there and made a promise that I haven't finished doing yet. I said, 'Lord, I will give half of my belongings to the poor. And I will repay four times over whatever I have taken wrongly from people.'"

"Wow," I said.

"And then Jesus said, 'Today salvation has come to this house. The Son of Man has come to seek out and save what was lost.' Do you understand what Jesus meant by that?"

"I think he meant that you were lost before because you were not living a good life," said Hannah. "And then you were saved because you turned your life around."

"Yes, so I am still going through my belongings and giving them away. Then I will sell this big house and live in a smaller one."

"But why are you giving back *four* times as much as you took? And why are you giving away half of your stuff?" I asked. I couldn't understand why he would do more than he had to, and how he could be so happy about it.

Zacchaeus put his head to one side, like he was thinking. Then he smiled.

"It is because I feel a great sense of responsibility," he said.

"You mean, you feel responsible to make up for what you did?"

"Yes, definitely. But I also feel a sense of responsibility for using well the gift Jesus gave me. He picked me. He could have ignored me up in the tree. I was not asking for help. I did not deserve to have him in my house. But he somehow knew I wanted more in my life and he picked me. And that's why I have to live differently. If I were to go back to my old life I would be wasting what he did for me."

Garrett had fallen asleep in Leah's arms.

"We should go now," she said.

"Wait!" said Zacchaeus. "I want to tell you something." He turned to Daniel. "I know how hard you have been working in the fields. I will help you find a tradesman who will take you as an apprentice."

"Oh!" said Daniel. "But—"

"I will pay off your debts and help support

you and your mother until you are ready to practice your trade. We can talk tomorrow about what you would like to do."

I looked at Leah. Her mouth was open and she started blinking back the tears.

"Oh, thank you!" said Daniel. He was smiling really big.

"Thank you," said Leah. "We can never pay you back for such generosity."

"I know," said Zacchaeus, smiling like a kid. "That is why I want to help you. I do not *want* to be paid back."

Chapter Twelve

An Important Question

Noah and Hannah and I went up to the roof to sleep. Daniel came with us, and Leah took care of Garrett.

"You guys," said Noah, "I'm sorry I ran away."

Hannah and I looked at each other.

"We know you're sorry," said Hannah, giving Noah a hug.

"I'm sorry, too, Noah," I said. "It was more my fault because I'm older. I knew you were upset, but I just made things worse."

"That's all right," said Noah. "You came and found me. And you, too, Daniel. Thanks!"

The next morning, the three of us knew we would soon be leaving.

"I think we should say good-bye to Leah and Daniel, so they don't think we are lost again," I said after we had had breakfast.

"Good idea," said Hannah.

We went to thank Leah and Daniel, and tell them that we were going out for a walk. We said we were probably going home today, so they shouldn't worry if they didn't see us.

Hannah walked with Garrett, holding his hand.

"Let's see if we can find the tree that Zacchaeus climbed," I said once we were walking down the street.

We went down the street toward the market where Zacchaeus said he had seen Jesus.

"I wonder if that's the tree," said Noah. "It would be fun to climb it!"

We all went toward it, and—you guessed it—we suddenly found ourselves moving in slow motion. We hadn't been going very fast because Garrett takes such little steps. But now it was as if the air had turned into water. Then,

just as suddenly, we were back in our own house, standing in the kitchen.

"Oh! Too bad!" said Noah.

"Well, we knew that would happen, right?" said Hannah.

"What were we doing before we left?" asked Noah.

We all looked at each other.

"Oh! You guys said you'd come play with Garrett and me, so I wouldn't be so bored."

"Cay!" said Garrett.

"What did he say? Is that your name, Caleb?" said Hannah.

"No, he calls me 'Cabe.'"

"Cay!" said Garrett, climbing onto a chair at the kitchen table.

"Yeah, we were going to ask Mom if we could get out some clay or finger paint," said Noah.

"Cay!"

"Oh, he's saying 'clay.' He remembered!" said Hannah.

"It was only five minutes ago," I said. "Why wouldn't he remember?

We all burst out laughing because it was true. But it was also true that it was two days ago!

That Sunday, we went to Mass as usual. In the reading from the Gospel, there was an interesting part where Jesus asked his disciples two questions.

The first question was, "Who do people say that I am?" Our priest, Father Joe, talked about it in his homily. He said the disciples told Jesus what they had heard some people say. Some people thought that Jesus was John the Baptist (even though he was dead), or that he was some new prophet.

"That was an easy question to answer," said Father Joe. "The next one was much harder."

The next question Jesus asked was, "Who do *you* say that I am?" He wanted to know what *each of them* thought, not what "some people" thought.

"This question was hard to answer because they had to take a stand," said Father Joe. "They had to say out loud what they believed. Maybe they were afraid to say it because then they would have to stand by what they had said and live up to it. Maybe they weren't so sure what they believed about Jesus.

"Jesus asks us this same question today," continued Father Joe. "He asks *me*, 'Who do you say I am, Joe?' He asks each of *you*, 'Who do you say that I am'—and here you can fill in your name. It's not enough to say what you were taught when you were a child, or to say what you've heard other people say. We have to be ready to say what we believe about Jesus. As adults, we each need to take responsibility for our faith. We need to know what we believe and witness to it.

"And the same with you kids," continued Father Joe. Here I perked up and looked over at Hannah and Noah. "Just because you're not grown-up yet doesn't mean Jesus isn't asking you this question, too. Yes, you are still learning your faith from your parents and others. But little by little you need to take responsibility for it. For example, as you get to know Jesus, you come to Mass because he invites you to, not because your parents make you. He asks you, also, 'Who do you say that I am?' How are you going to answer that?"

Well, that made me very excited. I liked the idea that Jesus was asking me and I needed to give the answer myself, not just say what someone told me to say.

I decided it was about time for me to be responsible not just for my chores and school work, but also for my faith. I tried to pay attention during the rest of Mass, even though I don't always understand the words Father Joe is praying. After Communion, I had a chance to talk to Jesus about it.

Jesus, I want to answer your question. This is who I say you are: You are my Good Shepherd. You are my friend. You are God and you can do miracles. You always love me, no matter what, and you always help me and forgive me when I do something wrong. You know what people are thinking and hoping. And you want everyone to be your friend.

I love you so much, Jesus! Help me be responsible for the things I'm supposed to do, even when I don't feel like it. I want to be your really good friend. And I'm not afraid to let everyone know!

Where Is It in the Bible?

In the four Gospels of Matthew, Mark, Luke, and John, there are several stories of Jesus giving sight to a blind man in different cities. Matthew, Mark, and Luke all have stories of Jesus healing a blind man at Jericho. Only the Gospel according to Mark tells us that the man's name was Bartimaeus. Here it is:

They came to Jericho. As he and his disciples and a large crowd were leaving Jericho, Bartimaeus son of Timaeus, a blind beggar, was sitting by the roadside. When he heard that it was Jesus of Nazareth, he began to shout out and say, "Jesus, Son of David, have mercy on me!" Many sternly ordered him to be quiet, but he cried out even more loudly, "Son of David, have mercy on me!" Jesus stood still and said, "Call him here." And they called the blind man, saying to him, "Take heart; get up, he is calling you." So throwing off his cloak, he sprang up and came to Jesus. Then Jesus said to him, "What do you want me to do for you?" The blind man said to him, "My teacher, let me see again." Jesus said to him, "Go; your faith has made you well." Immediately he regained his sight and followed him on the way (Mark 10:46–52).

The story of Zacchaeus is only found in the Gospel according to Luke. It comes right after Luke's version of the story of the blind man:

He entered Jericho and was passing through it. A man was there named Zacchaeus; he was a chief tax collector and was rich. He was trying to see who Jesus was, but on account of the crowd he could not, because he was short in stature. So he ran ahead and climbed a sycamore tree to see him, because he was going to pass that way. When Jesus came to the place, he looked up and said to him, "Zacchaeus, hurry and come down; for I must stay at your house today." So he hurried down and was happy to welcome him. All who saw it began to grumble and said, "He has gone to be the guest of one who is a sinner." Zacchaeus stood there and said to the Lord, "Look, half of my possessions, Lord, I will give to the poor; and if I have defrauded anyone of anything, I will pay back four times as much." Then Jesus said to him, "Today salvation has come to this house, because he too is a son of Abraham. For the Son of Man came to seek out and to save the lost" (Luke 19:1–10).

BOOKS & MEDIA

The Daughters of St. Paul operate book and media centers at the following addresses. Visit, call, or write the one nearest you today, or find us at www.pauline.org.

CALIFORNIA
3908 Sepulveda Blvd, Culver City, CA 90230   310-397-8676
935 Brewster Avenue, Redwood City, CA 94063   650-369-4230
5945 Balboa Avenue, San Diego, CA 92111   858-565-9181

FLORIDA
145 SW 107th Avenue, Miami, FL 33174   305-559-6715

HAWAII
1143 Bishop Street, Honolulu, HI 96813   808-521-2731
Neighbor Islands call: 866-521-2731

ILLINOIS
172 North Michigan Avenue, Chicago, IL 60601   312-346-4228

LOUISIANA
4403 Veterans Memorial Blvd, Metairie, LA 70006   504-887-7631

MASSACHUSETTS
885 Providence Hwy, Dedham, MA 02026   781-326-5385

MISSOURI
9804 Watson Road, St. Louis, MO 63126   314-965-3512

NEW YORK
64 West 38th Street, New York, NY 10018   212-754-1110

PENNSYLVANIA
Philadelphia—relocating   215-676-9494

SOUTH CAROLINA
243 King Street, Charleston, SC 29401   843-577-0175

VIRGINIA
1025 King Street, Alexandria, VA 22314   703-549-3806

CANADA
3022 Dufferin Street, Toronto, ON M6B 3T5   416-781-9131